USBORNE FIRST READING

Level Four

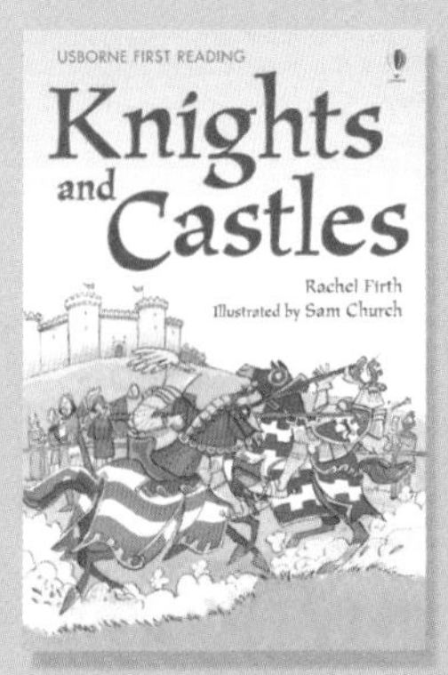

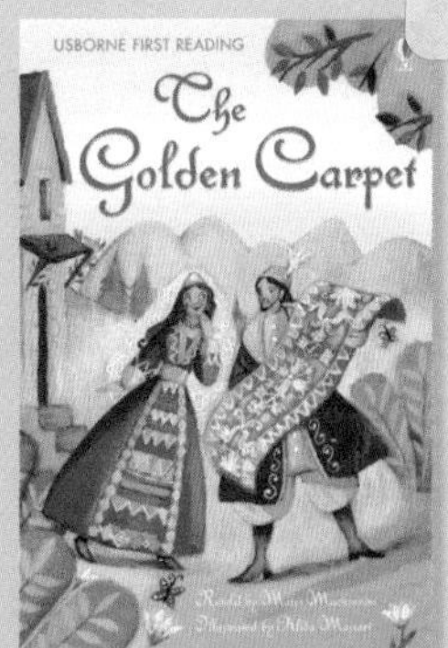

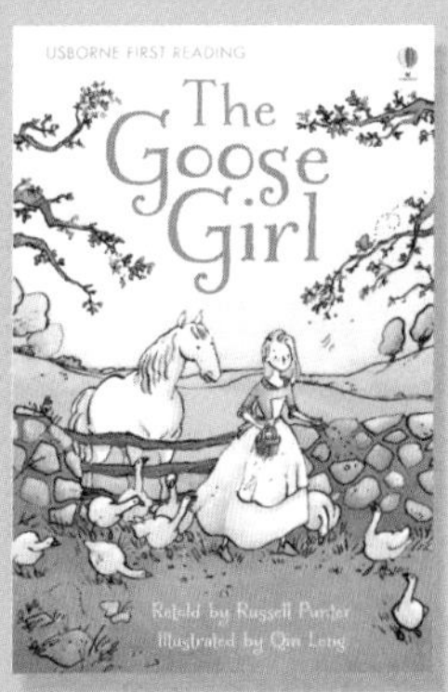

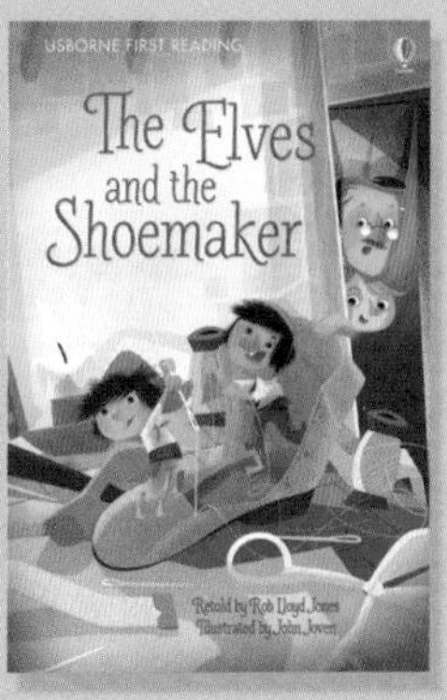

The Story of Pinocchio

by Carlo Collodi

Retold by Andy Prentice
Illustrated by Jesús Lopez

Reading consultant: Alison Kelly

Once upon a time, there was a piece of wood.

It stood in the workshop of Gepetto, the wood carver.

One day Gepetto said,
"I think I'll make a puppet.
I will call him Pinocchio!"

He had almost finished when... the puppet's nose grew!

Gepetto cut it off.

It grew even longer.

Gepetto shook his head. "I must be tired," he thought. "Time for bed."

That night, something magical happened...

Pinocchio came to life!
Suddenly, he could talk.

He could laugh and sing.
He could jump and dance.

The noise woke up Gepetto. "You're alive?" he cried.

He had always wanted a child. A talking puppet was almost as good.

But Pinocchio was the naughtiest puppet. He didn't like doing what he was told.

He refused to tidy up and he was *always* playing tricks.

Gepetto loved him so much, he never once got cross.

Alfred, a cricket who lived in the workshop, was shocked.

"Be quiet!" shouted Pinocchio, hurling a book.

Poor Alfred. The book hit him hard and he died. Pinocchio just shrugged.

Alfred became a ghost cricket.

After that, only Pinocchio could see Alfred.

"I haven't seen him for ages," lied Pinocchio...

...and something funny happened. His nose grew!

The more Pinocchio lied, the longer his nose grew.

Gepetto frowned.

Pinocchio grew scared and
ran out of the house.

He bumped into a grinning fox. “Are you going to the puppet show?” asked the fox.

“There’s a puppet show?” said Pinocchio. “I want to see that.”

Pinocchio didn't have any money for a ticket.

So he sneaked inside.

The show was amazing. Then the puppets saw Pinocchio in the crowd.

"Hello, Puppet!" one called out and the show stopped.

"Another puppet!" cried the puppet master. "You must join my show."

He chased after Pinocchio. Pinocchio ran and ran into the forest.

"Help!" panted Pinocchio. The puppet master had almost reached him.

Just then, a door opened in a tree.

Pinocchio ducked inside.

There stood a Blue Fairy.
She was not happy.

"But at least I'm safe now," thought Pinocchio.

The kind Blue Fairy made Pinocchio an incredible promise.
If you go home, and behave...
...you will become a real boy.

"I'll go home soon," thought Pinocchio, as he left.

Outside the tree, he saw the fox.

"Why don't you visit Toyland?" said the fox. "It's perfect for puppets."

"Toyland sounds fun!" said Pinocchio.

He stole a boat and rowed as hard as he could.

Back in his workshop, Gepetto decided to look for Pinocchio.

He built a boat, filled it with supplies and set out.

But a terrible dogfish swallowed him and his boat in one

big

gulp.

In Toyland, Pinocchio was having a wonderful time.

Every day was a holiday.

He could eat ice cream whenever he wanted...

...and play with his friends all day. There was no bedtime.

Sometimes his friends didn't come to play.

Pinocchio was having too much fun to worry.

Then, one dreadful morning, he woke up with donkey's ears.

Pinocchio was terrified.

By the evening, Pinocchio had completely turned into a donkey.

Pinocchio burst into tears.

The Blue Fairy heard him sobbing.

She waved her wand... and he was a puppet again.

She gave Pinocchio a boat and he went to sea.

He couldn't wait to see his father.

But the terrible dogfish had other ideas.

It swallowed Pinocchio and his boat in one big gulp...

...and there was Gepetto! He had built a lovely home inside the fish.

Pinocchio ran to his father for a hug.

"Now we need to get out of here," Pinocchio said.

Luckily, the dogfish
was ticklish.

It started to sneeze and
they shot out...

...into a storm.

The wind howled. The waves were like mountains and it was very, very cold.

When they arrived home, Gepetto was sick.

Pinocchio took care of him. He cooked every meal.

He found a job so he could buy medicine. The work was hard and the days were long.

Pinocchio didn't complain.
He just worked.

Finally, Gepetto was better.
It was the happiest day of
Pinocchio's life.

That night, the Blue Fairy came to visit Pinocchio.

"I'm so proud of you," she whispered.

When Pinocchio woke up, something magical had happened...

...and Pinocchio, Gepetto and Alfred lived happily ever after.

About Pinocchio

Pinocchio first appeared in a magazine for children. In 1883, his adventures were published in a book. Pinocchio's tale is one of the best-selling stories ever written.

Designed by Laura Nelson Norris
Series editor: Lesley Sims
Series designer: Russell Punter
Digital imaging: Nick Wakeford

First published in 2021 by Usborne Publishing Ltd., Usborne House, 83-85 Saffron Hill, London EC1N 8RT, England. usborne.com

USBORNE FIRST READING
Level Four

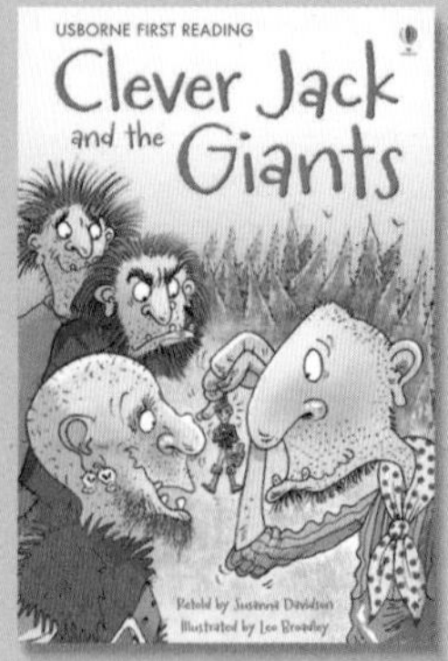

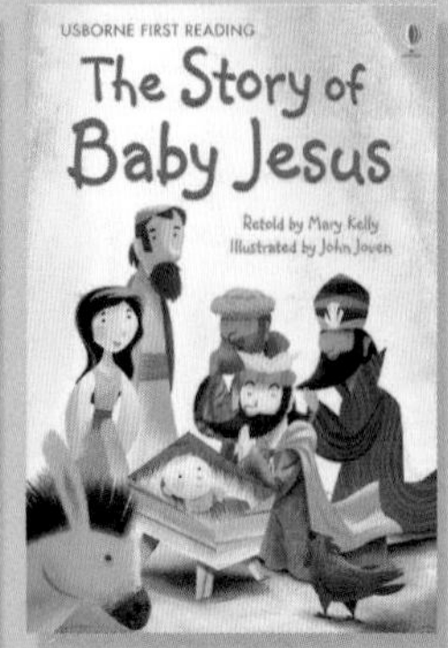